SILLY LILLY

AND THE FOUR SEASONS

Agnès Rosenstiehl

SILLY LILLY

AND THE FOUR SEASONS

A TOON BOOK BY

Agnès Rosenstiehl

THE LITTLE LIT LIBRARY, A DIVISION OF RAW JUNIOR, LLC, NEW YORK

for Roro

Editorial Director: FRANÇOISE MOULY
Advisor: ART SPIEGELMAN

Book Design: FRANÇOISE MOULY & JONATHAN BENNETT

Copyright © 2008 RAW Junior, LLC, 27 Greene Street, New York, NY 10013.
Printed in Singapore by Tien Wah Press (Pte.) Ltd. No part of this book may be used or
reproduced in any manner whatsoever without written permission except in the case of brief
quotations embodied in critical articles and reviews. TOON Books, LITTLE LIT® and
THE LITTLE LIT LIBRARY are trademarks of RAW Junior, LLC. All rights reserved.
Library of Congress Control Number: 2007941869
ISBN 13: 978-0-9799238-7-6 ISBN 10: 0-9799238-7-5
Paperback Edition
10 9 8 7 6 5 4 3 2

WWW.TOON-BOOKS.COM

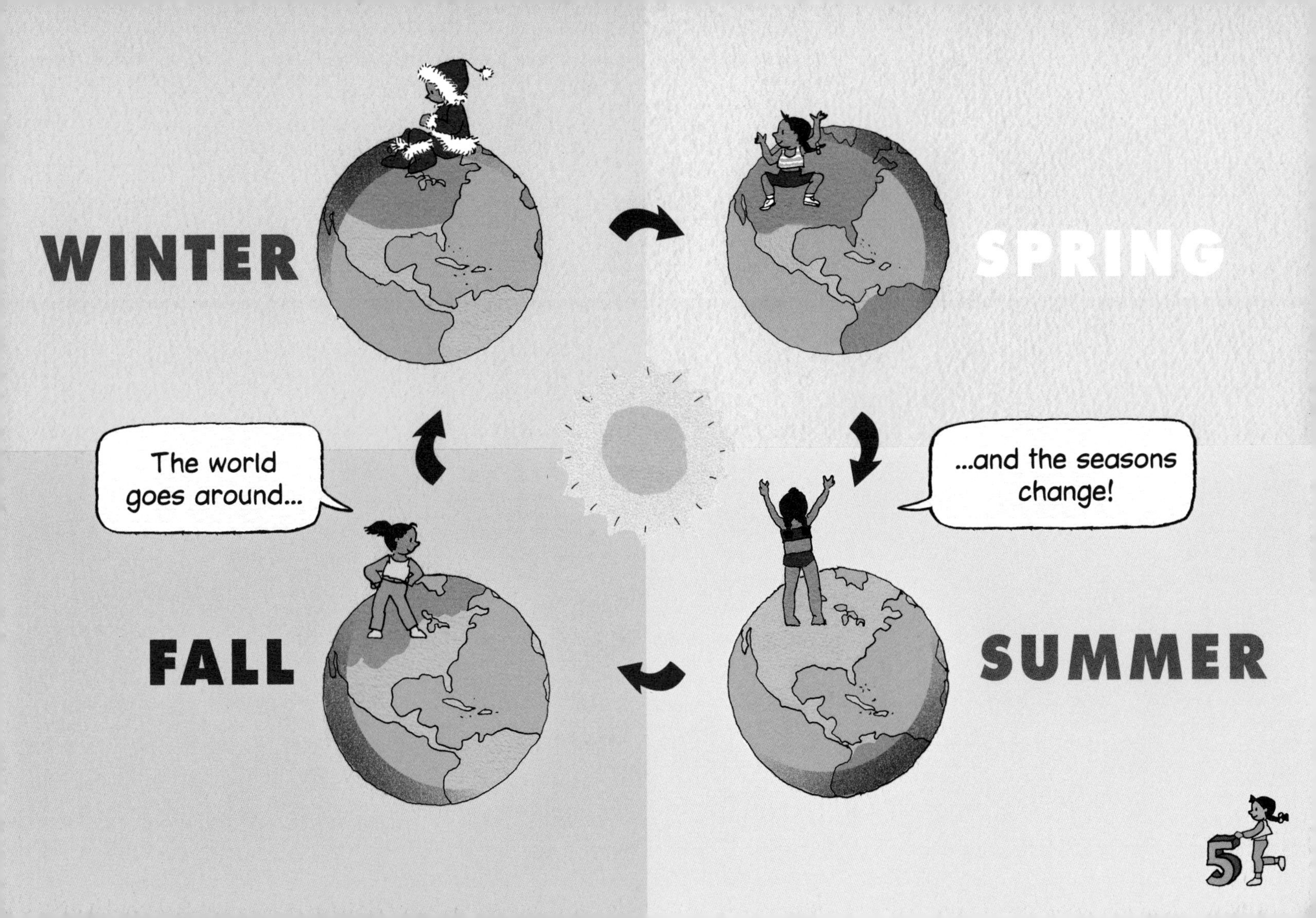
WINTER
SPRING
The world goes around...
...and the seasons change!
FALL
SUMMER

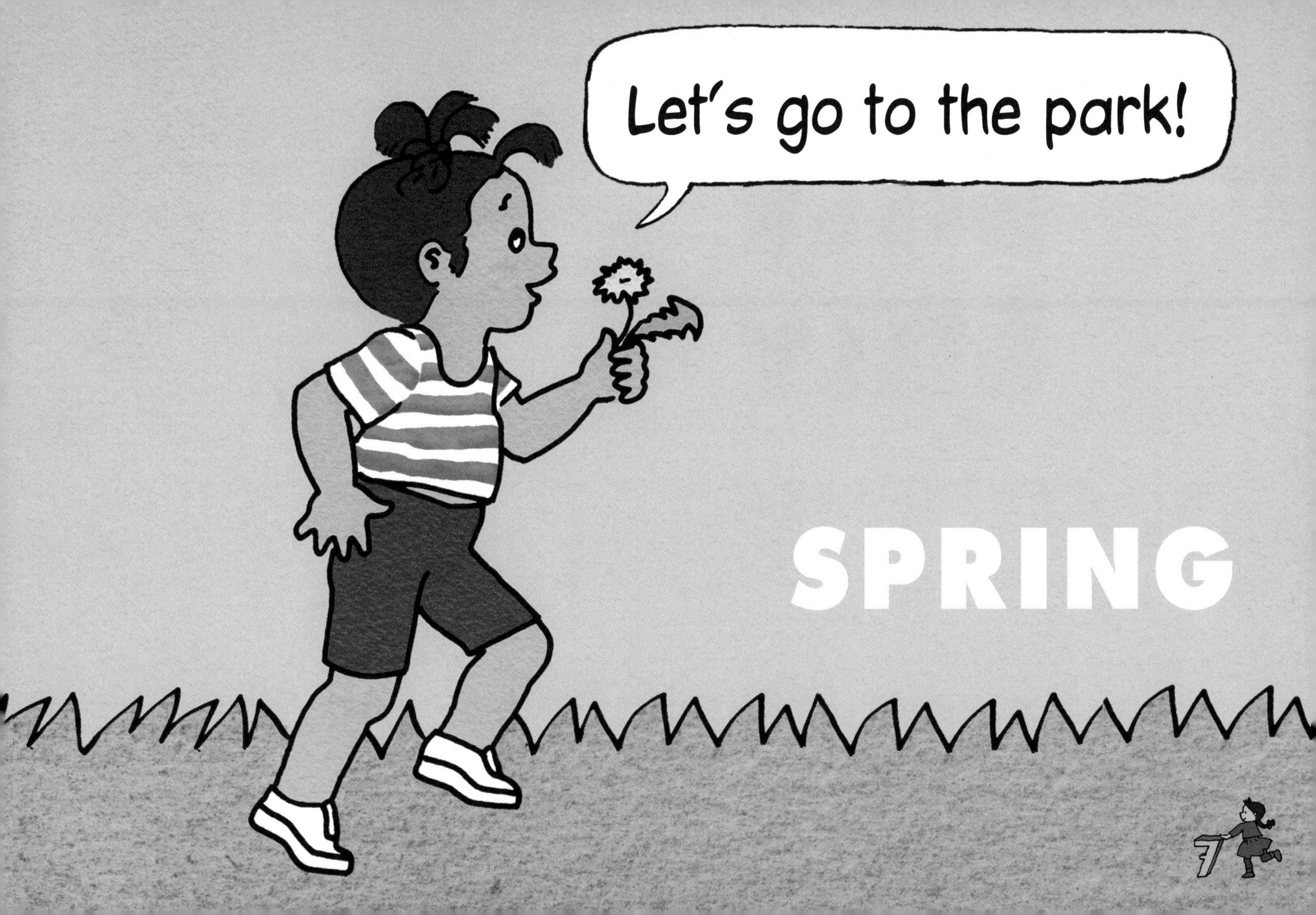
Let's go to the park!
SPRING

SILLY LILLY

AT THE PARK

There is so much to do at the park!

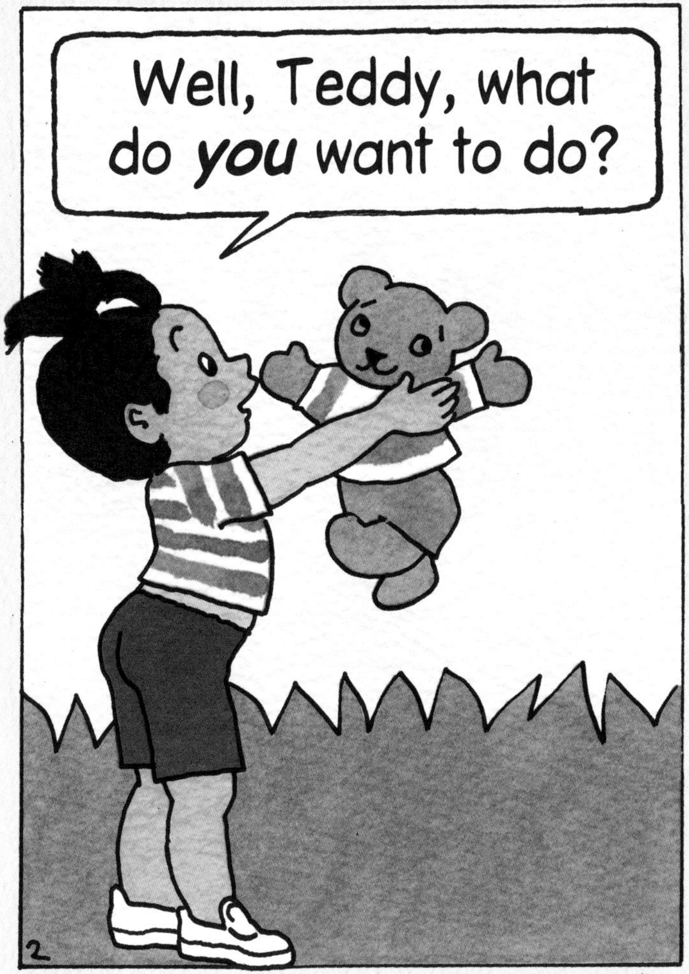
Well, Teddy, what do *you* want to do?
2

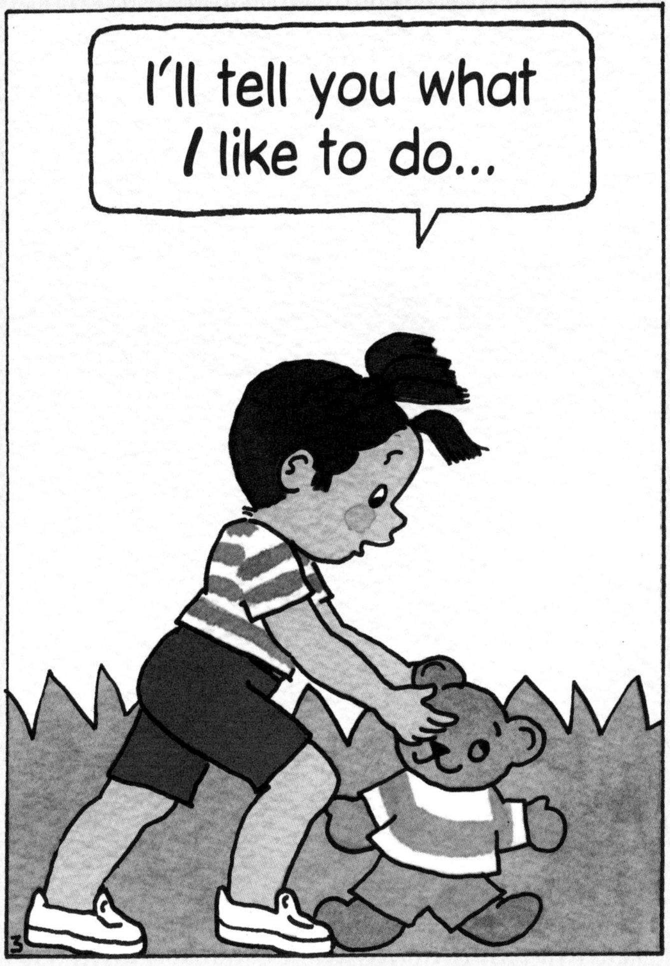
I'll tell you what *I* like to do...
3

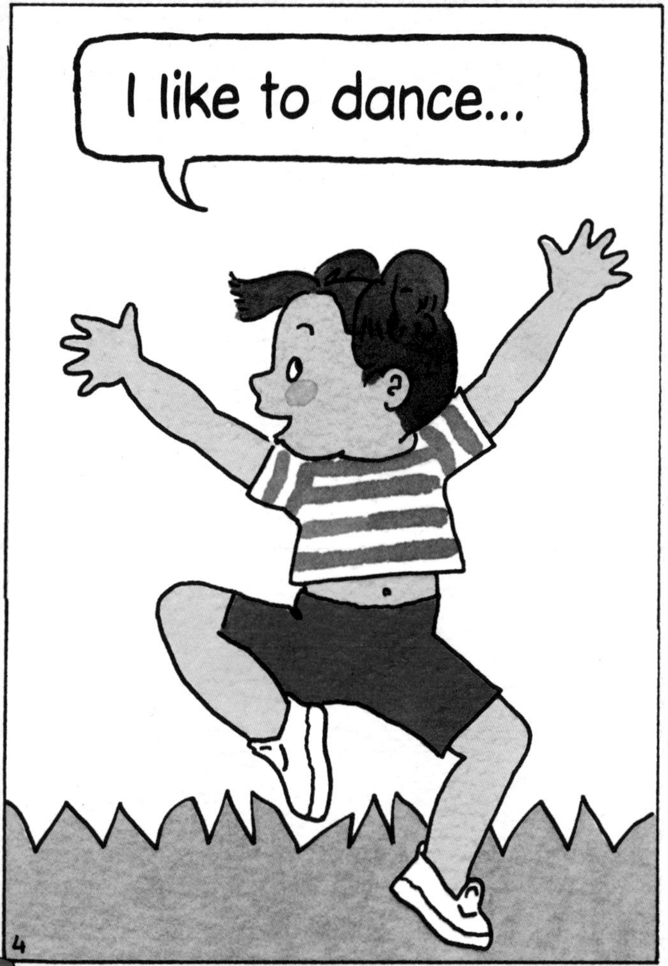
I like to dance...
4

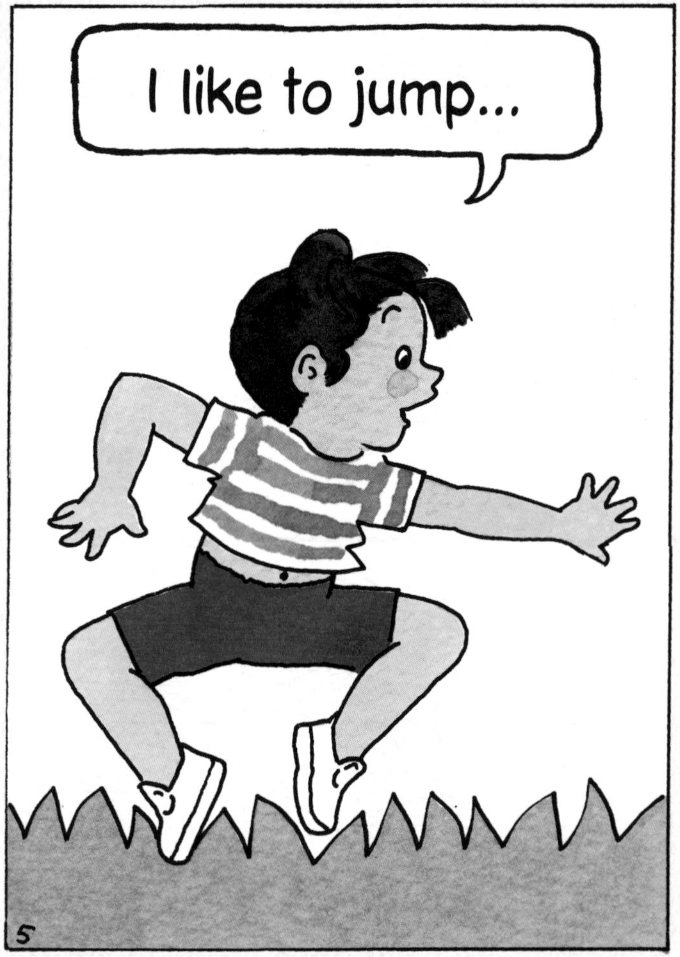
I like to jump...
5

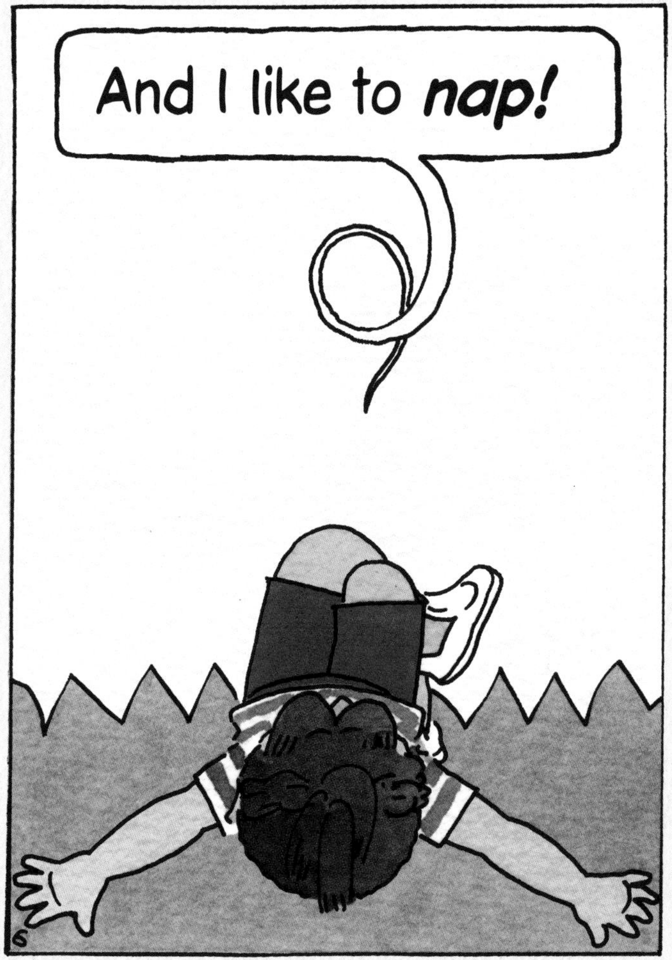
And I like to *nap!*
6

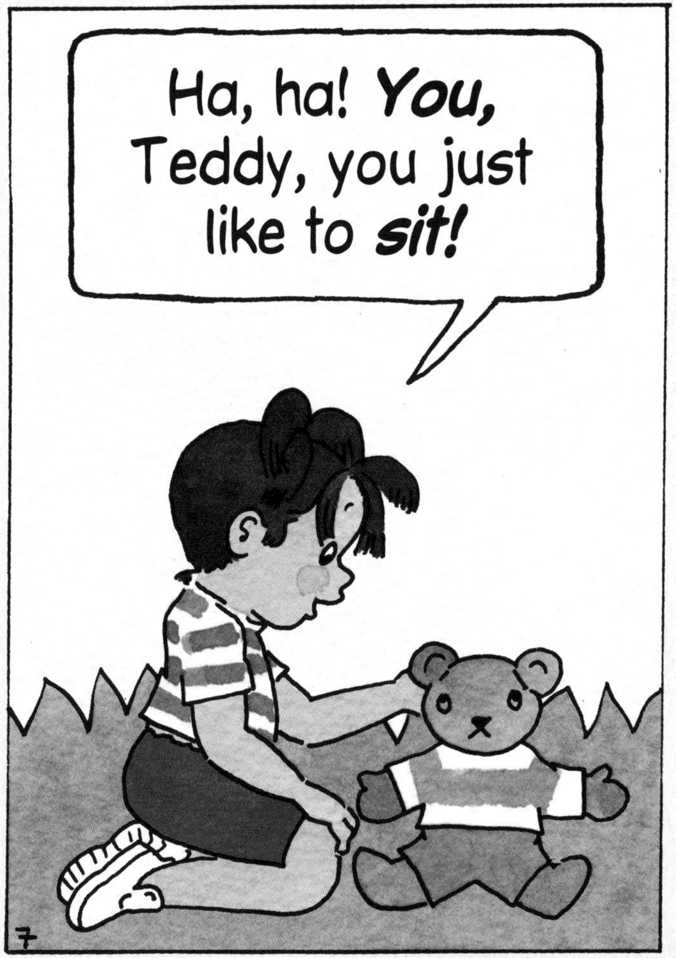
Ha, ha! ***You,*** Teddy, you just like to ***sit!***
7

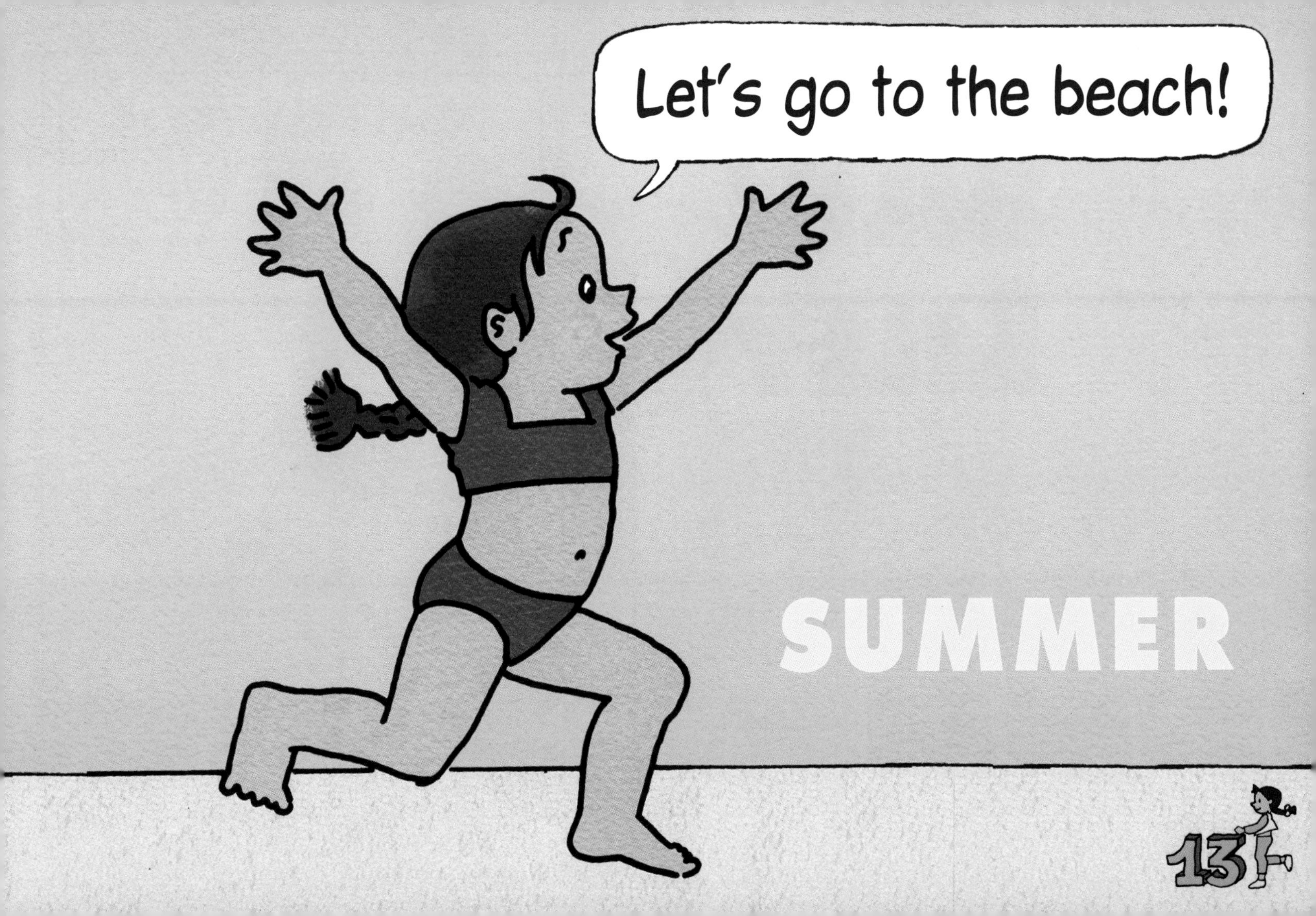
Let's go to the beach!
SUMMER

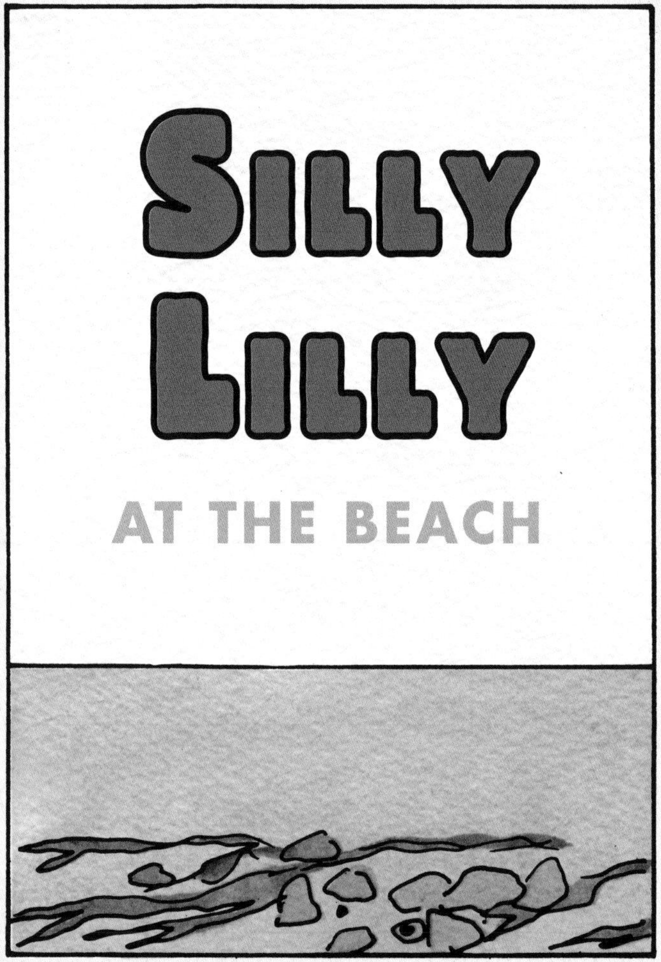
SILLY
LILLY
AT THE BEACH

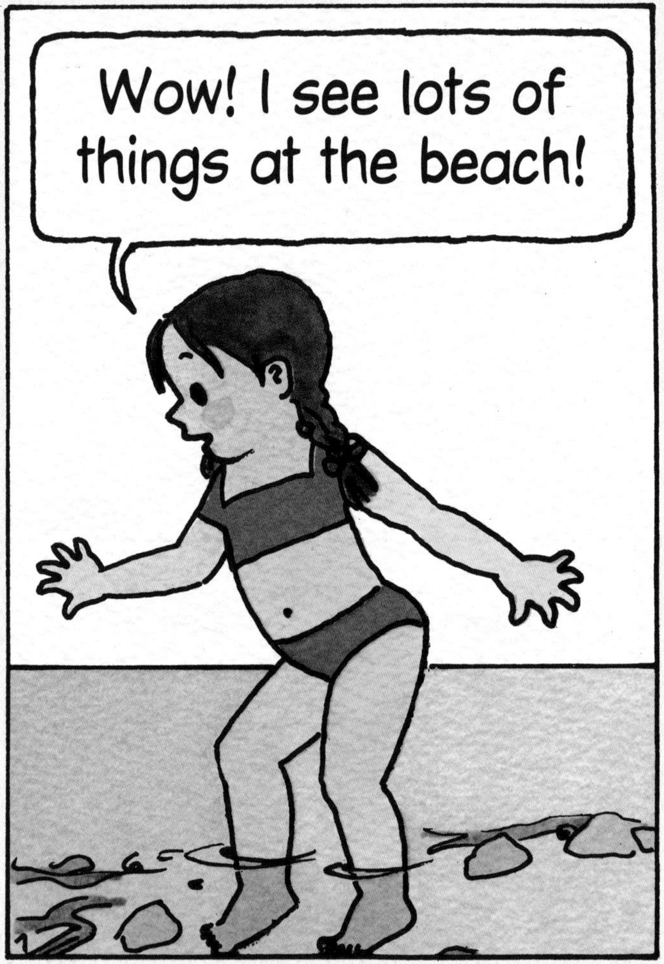
Wow! I see lots of things at the beach!

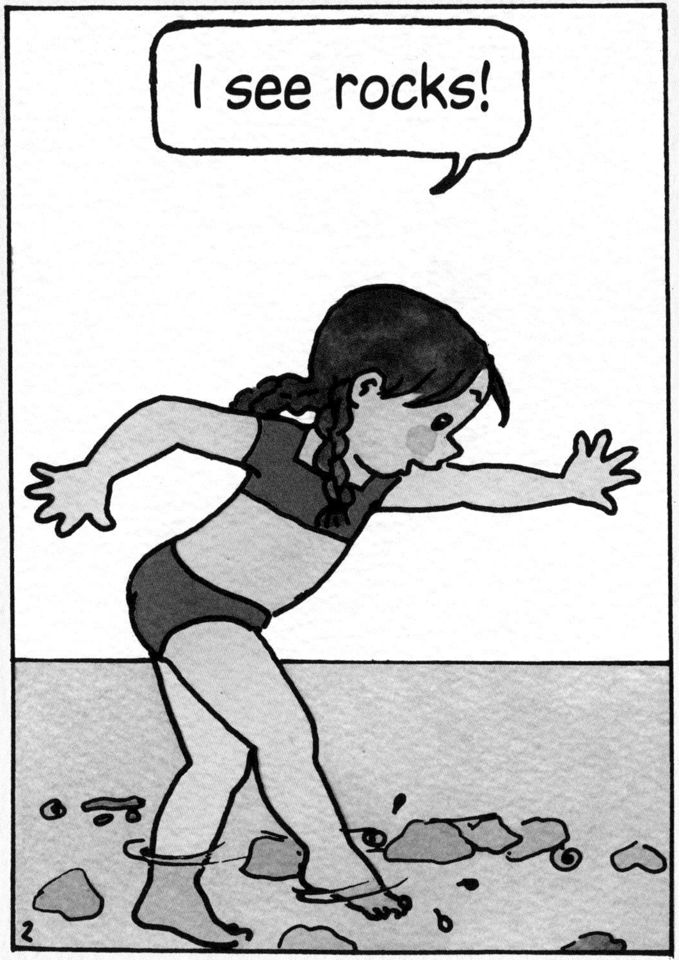
I see rocks!

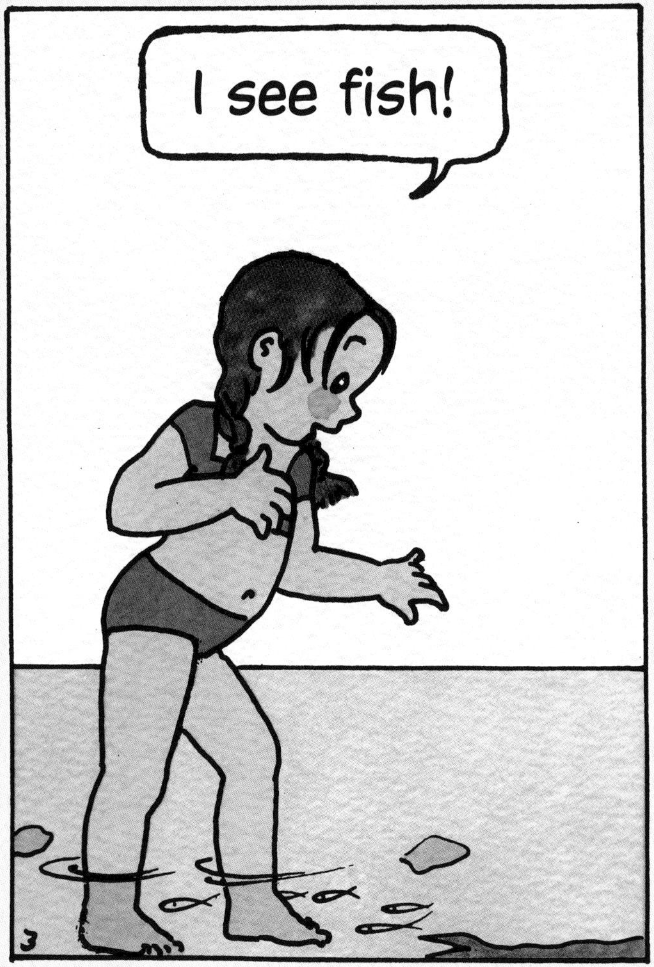
I see fish!

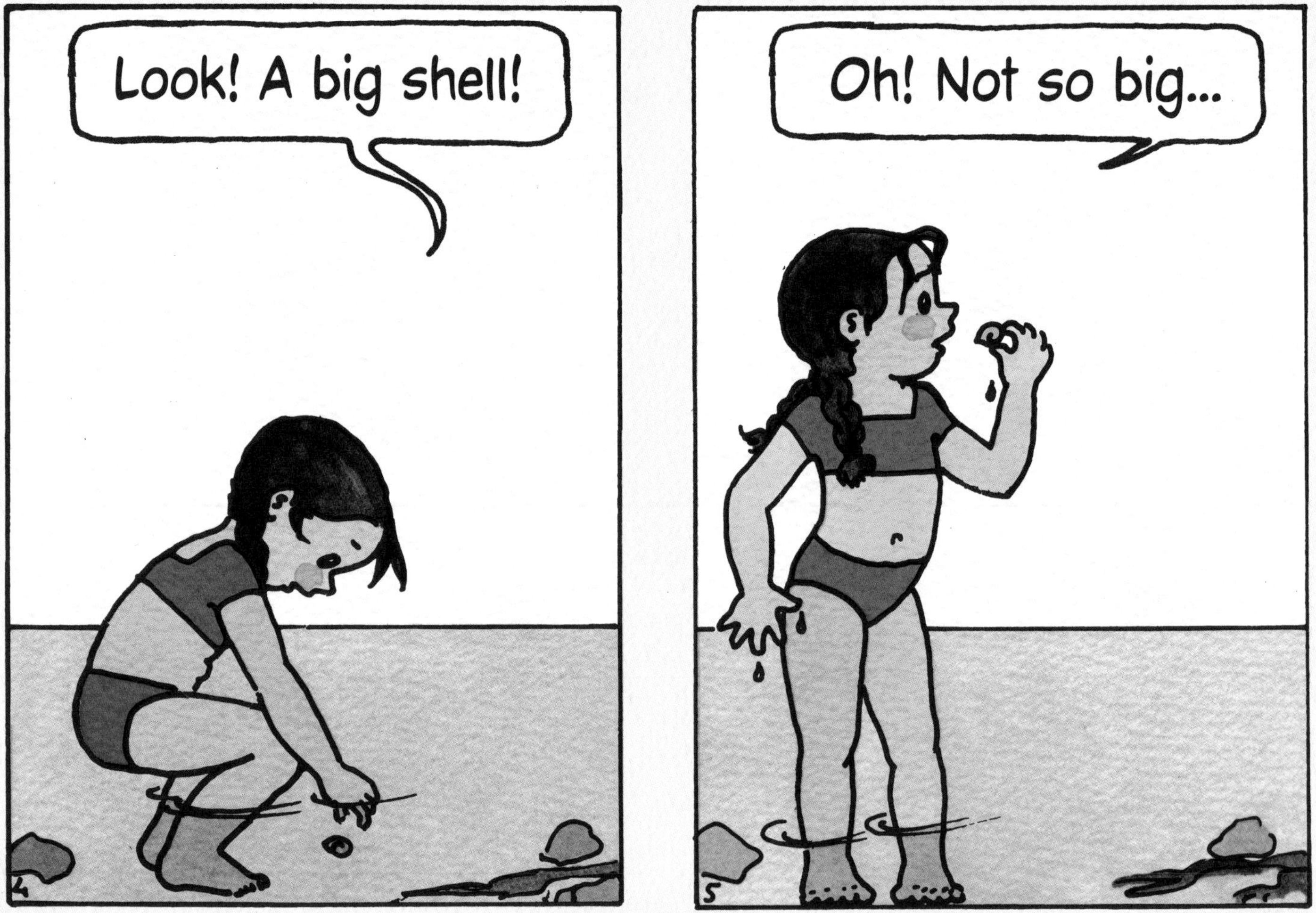
Look! A big shell!
Oh! Not so big...

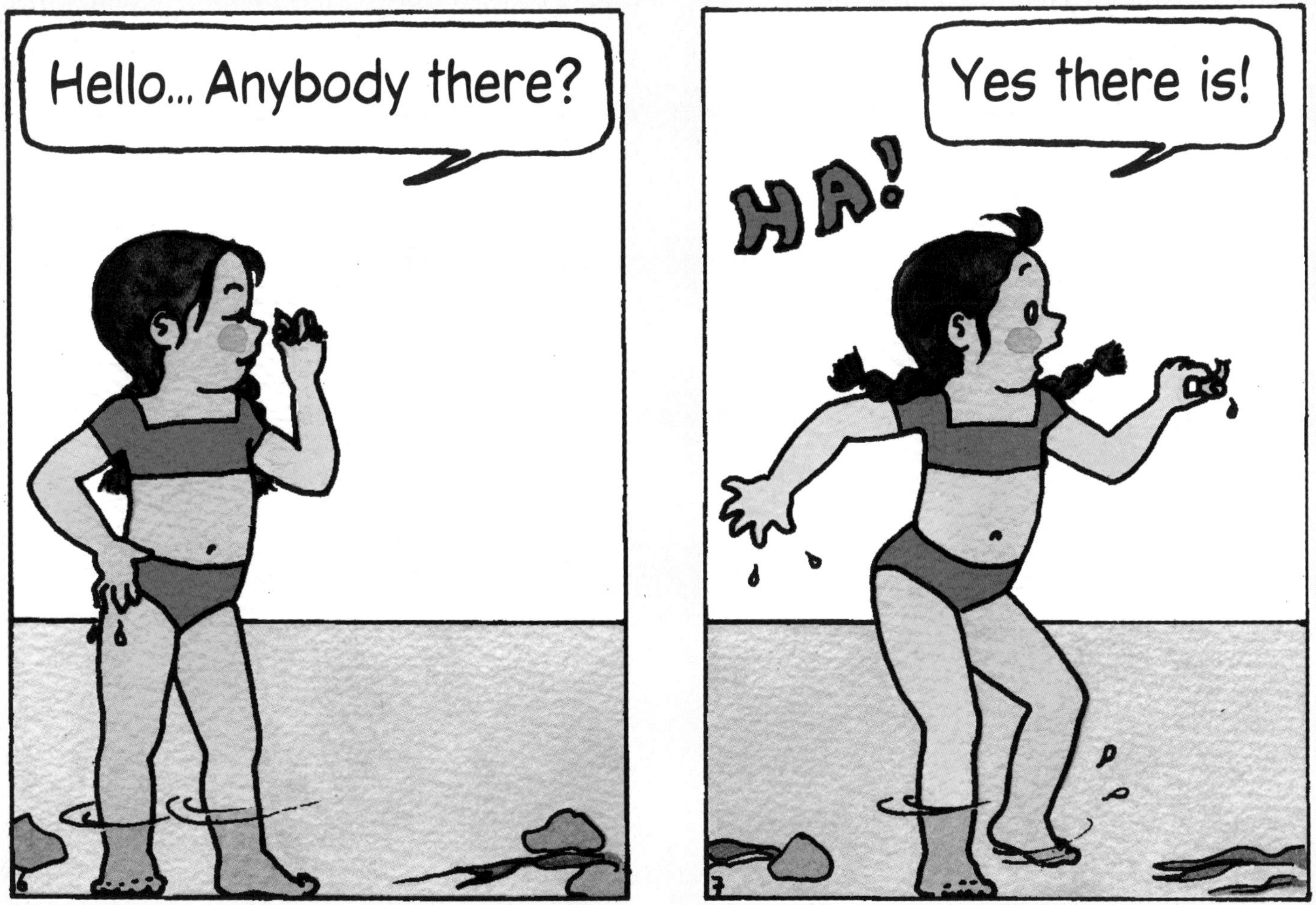
Hello... Anybody there?
HA!
Yes there is!

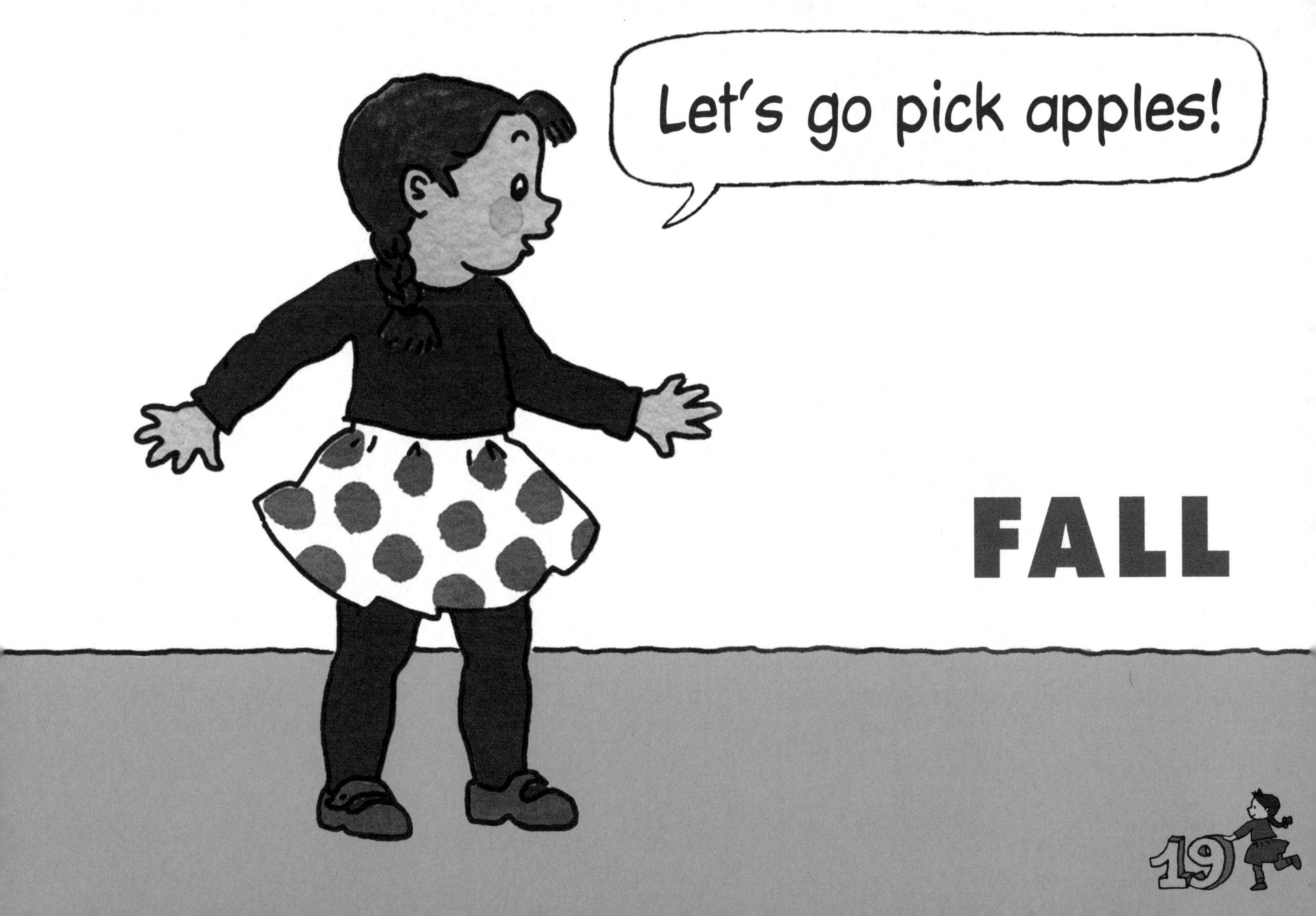
Let's go pick apples!
FALL

SILLY LILLY

AND

THE APPLES

Wow!
Look at all the apples!

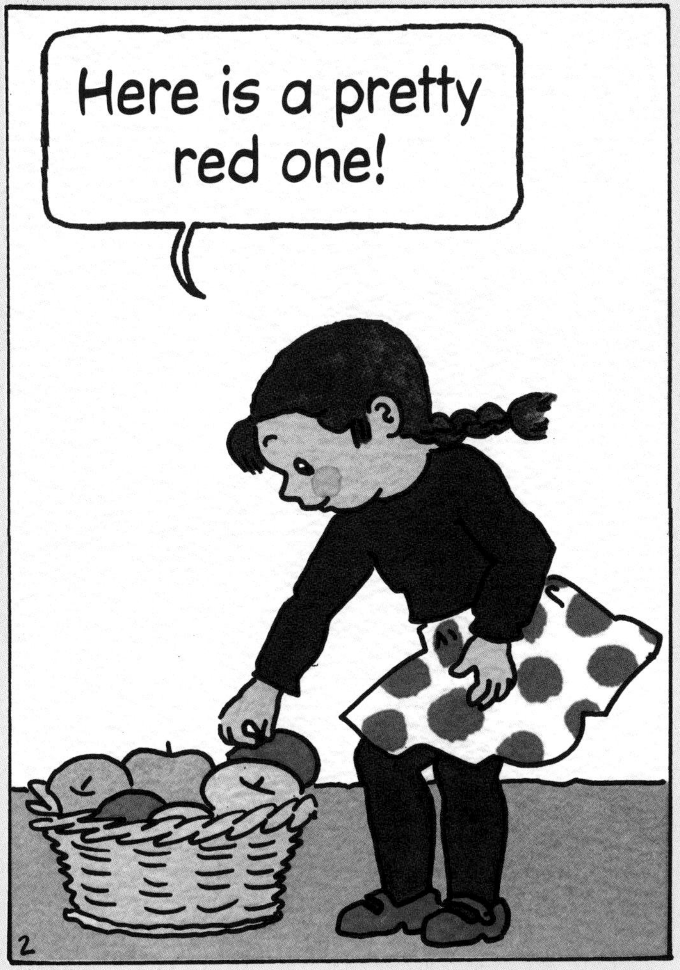
Here is a pretty red one!
2

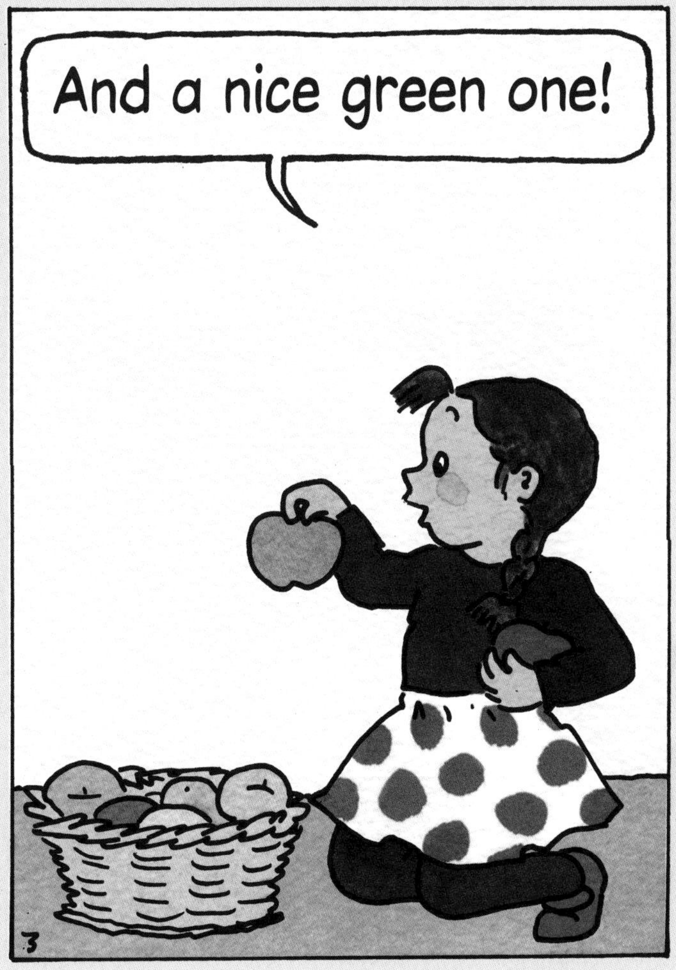
And a nice green one!
3

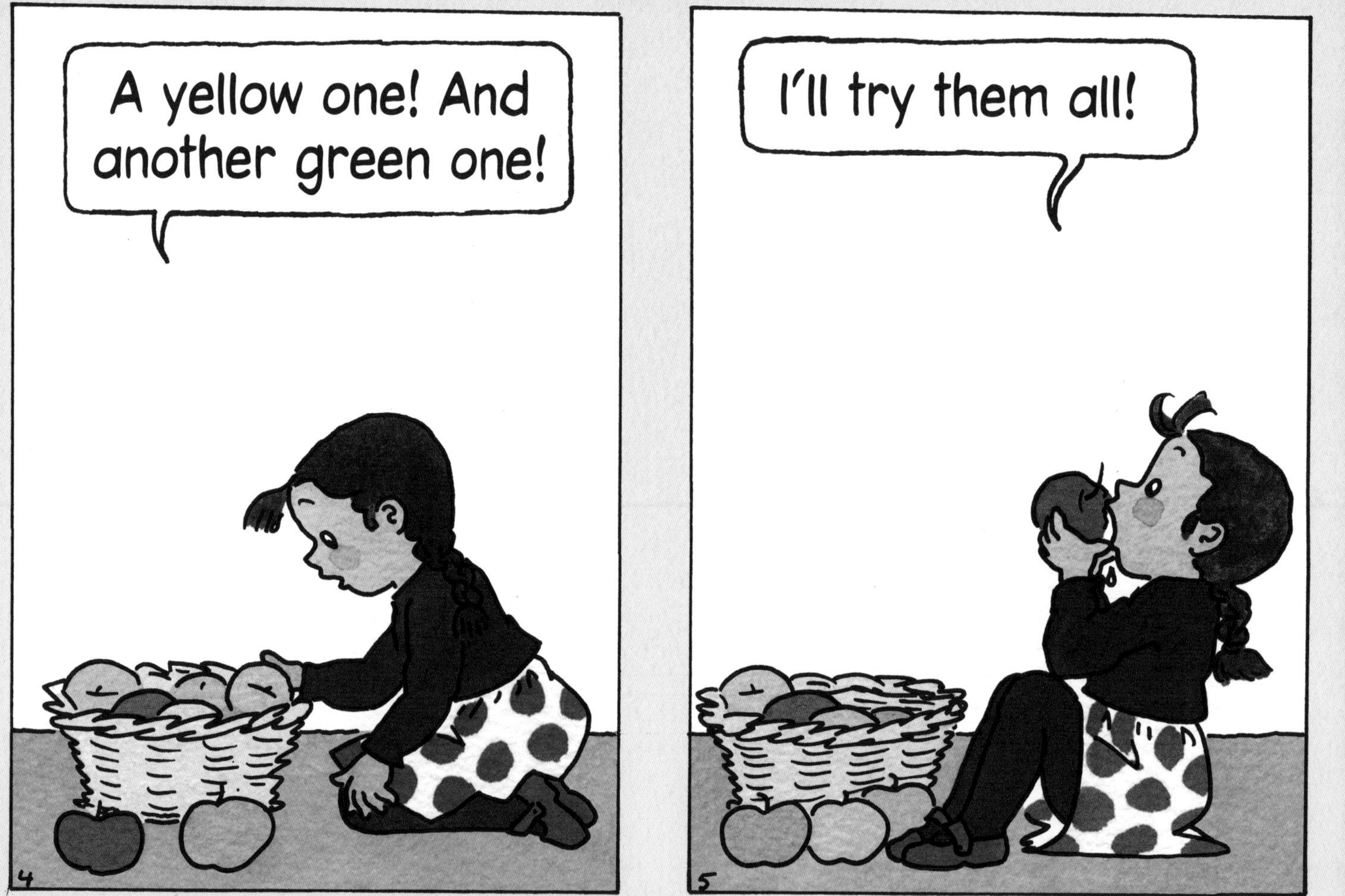
A yellow one! And another green one!
I'll try them all!

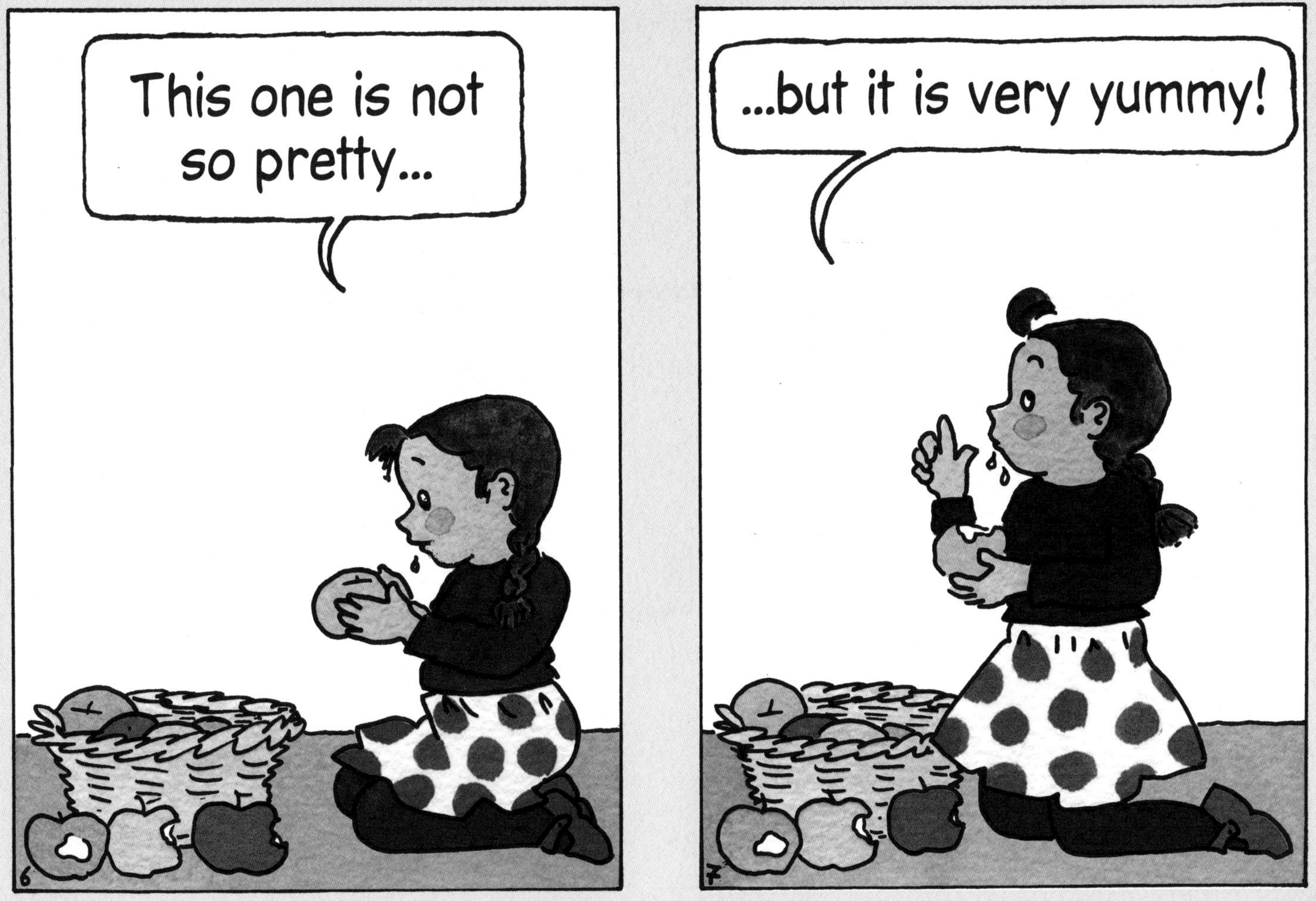
This one is not so pretty...
...but it is very yummy!

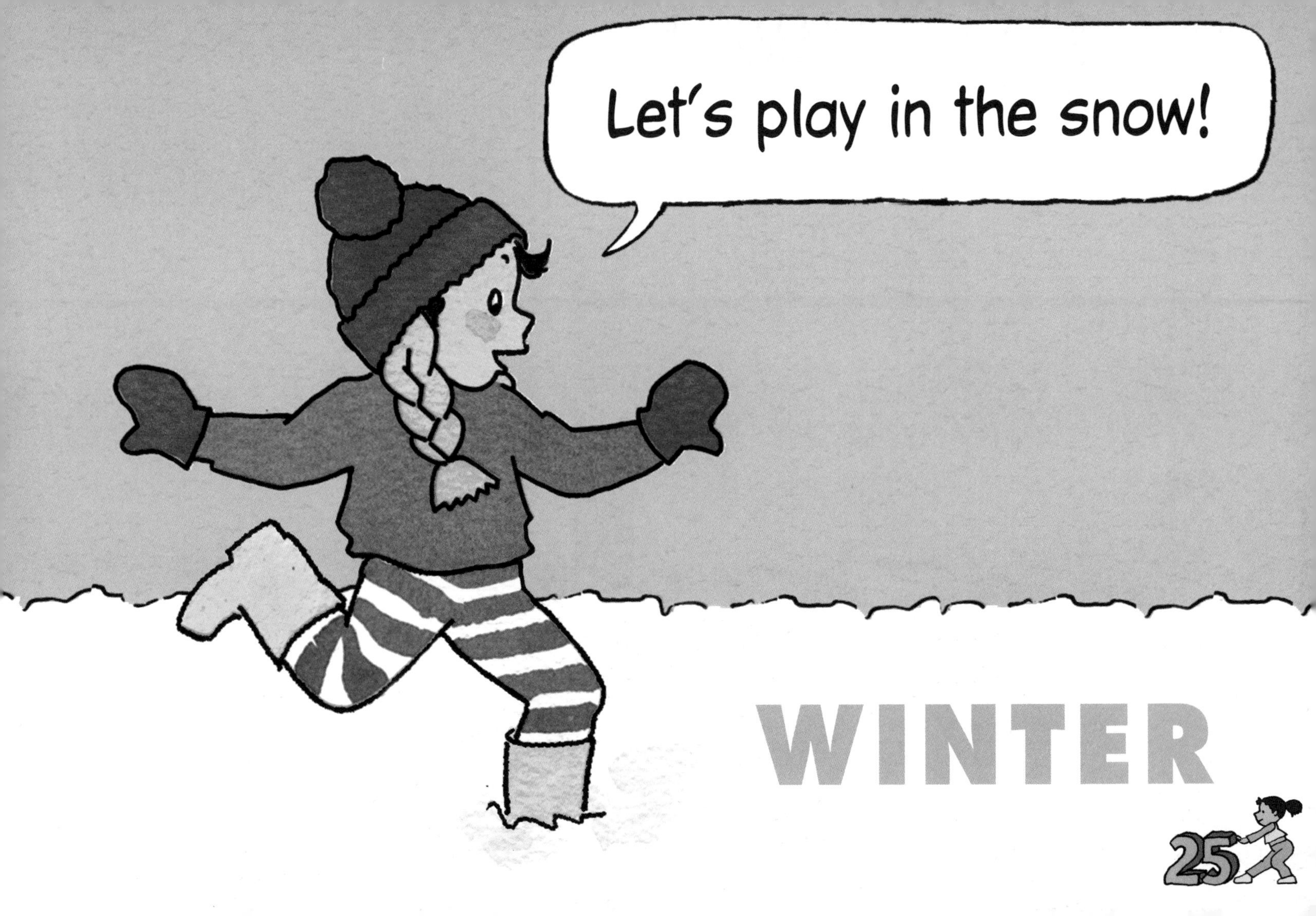
Let's play in the snow!
WINTER

SILLY LILLY

PLAYS IN THE SNOW

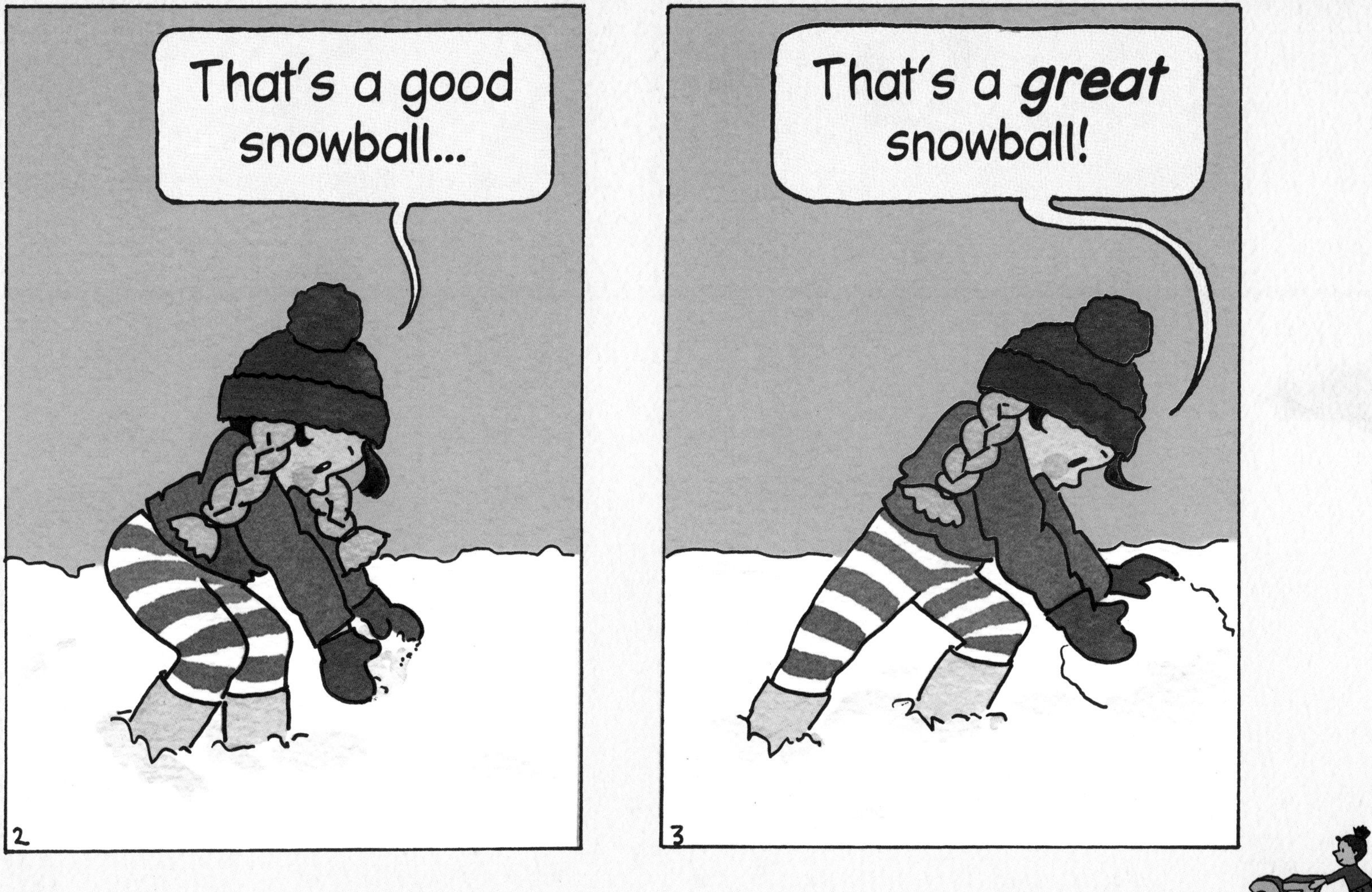

2
That's a good snowball...
3
That's a great snowball!

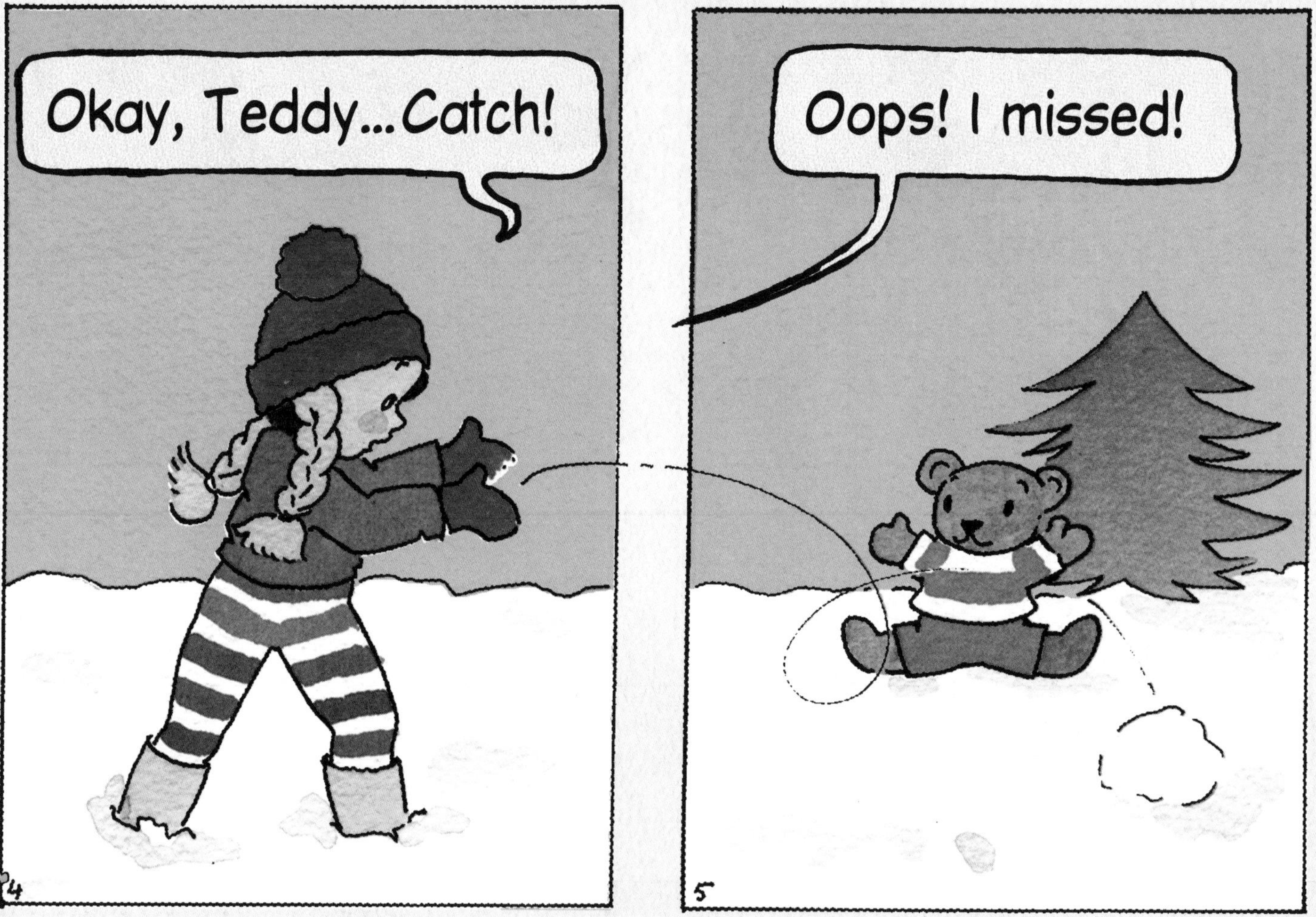
Okay, Teddy...Catch!
4
Oops! I missed!
5

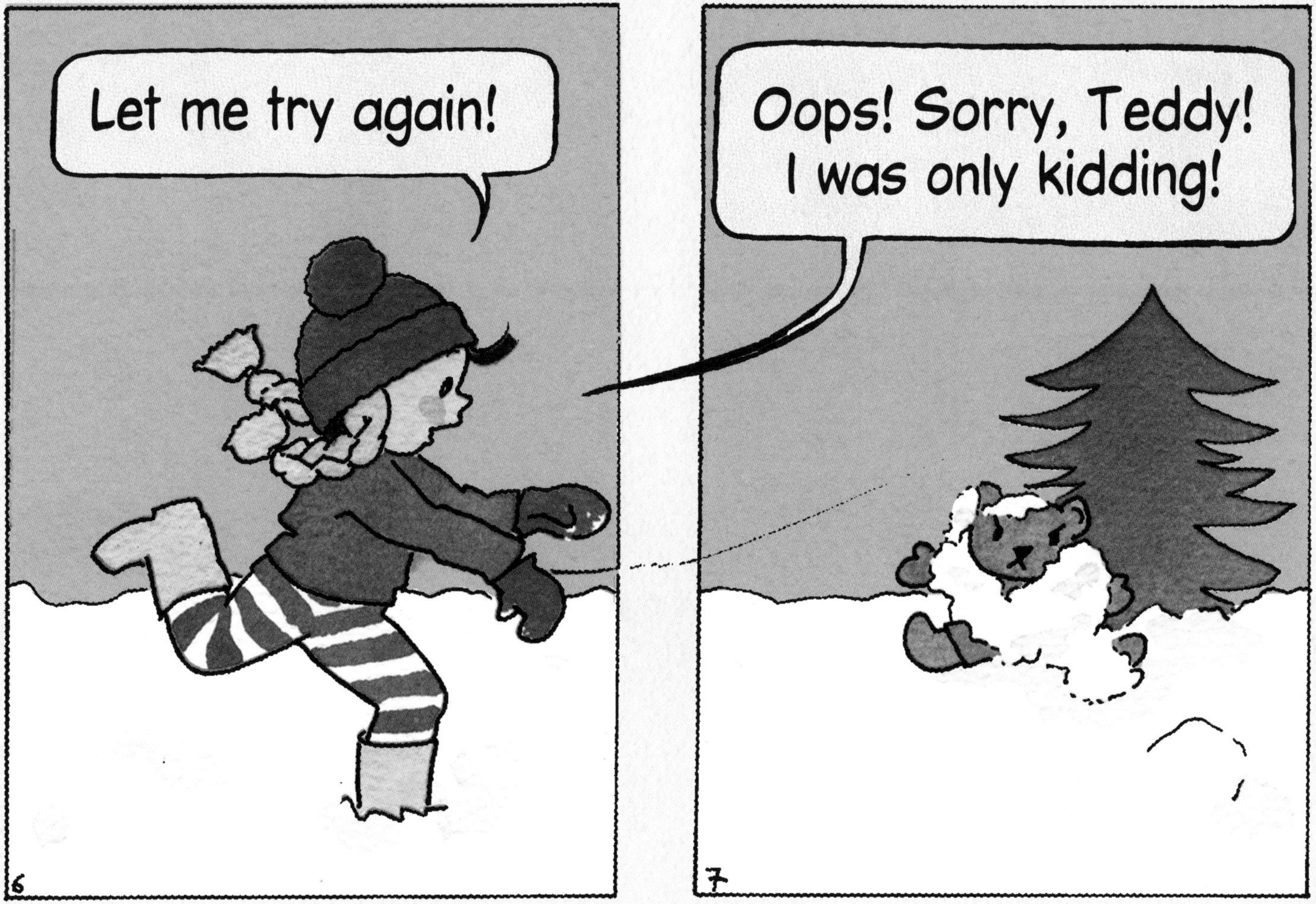
6
Let me try again!
7
Oops! Sorry, Teddy! I was only kidding!

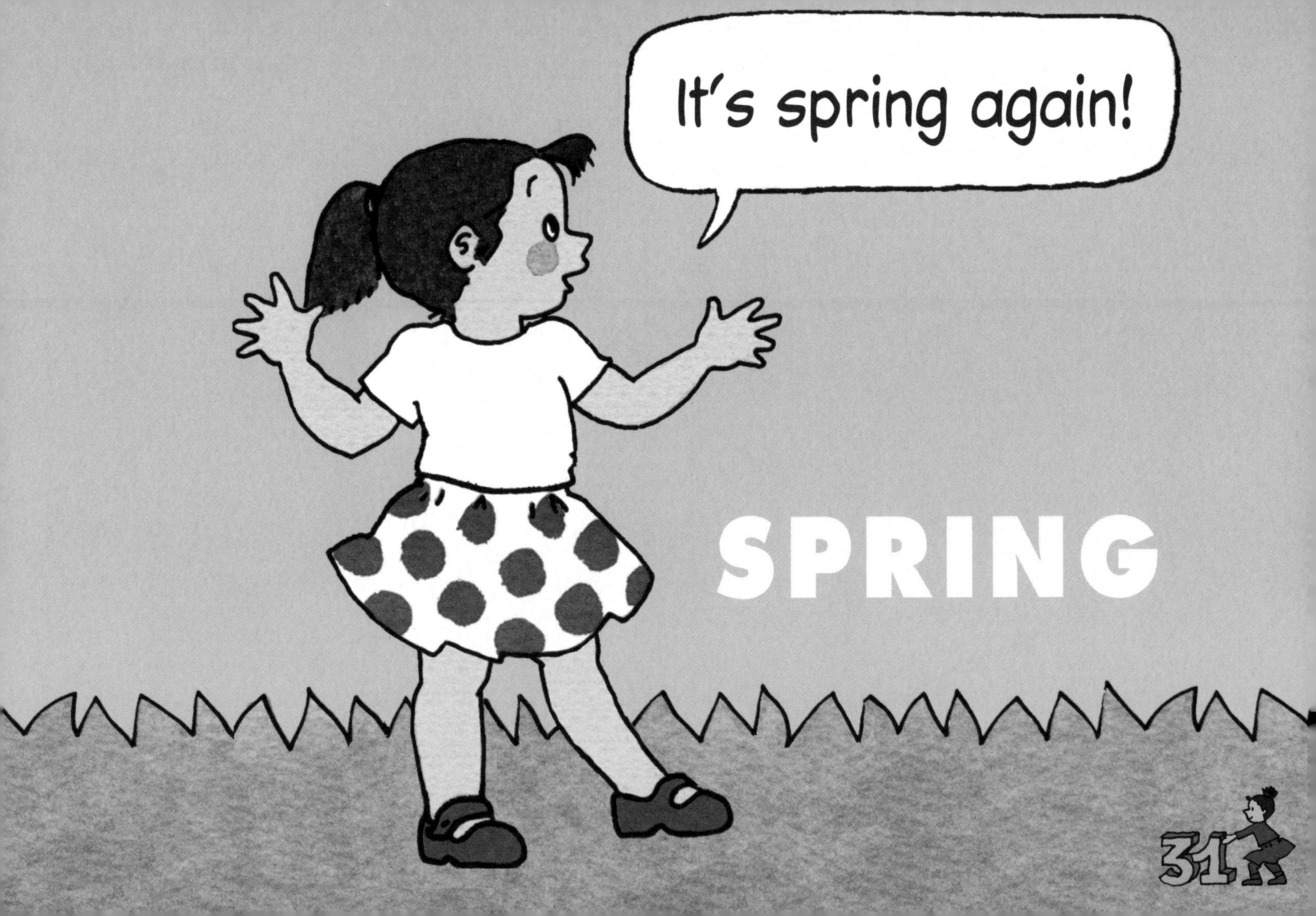
It's spring again!
SPRING

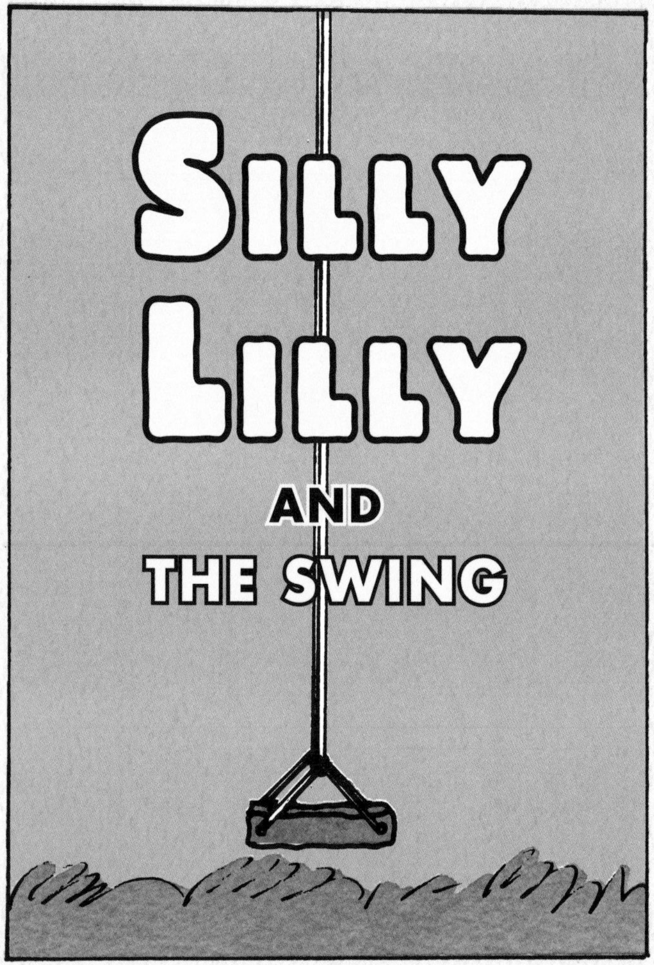
SILLY
LILLY
AND
THE SWING

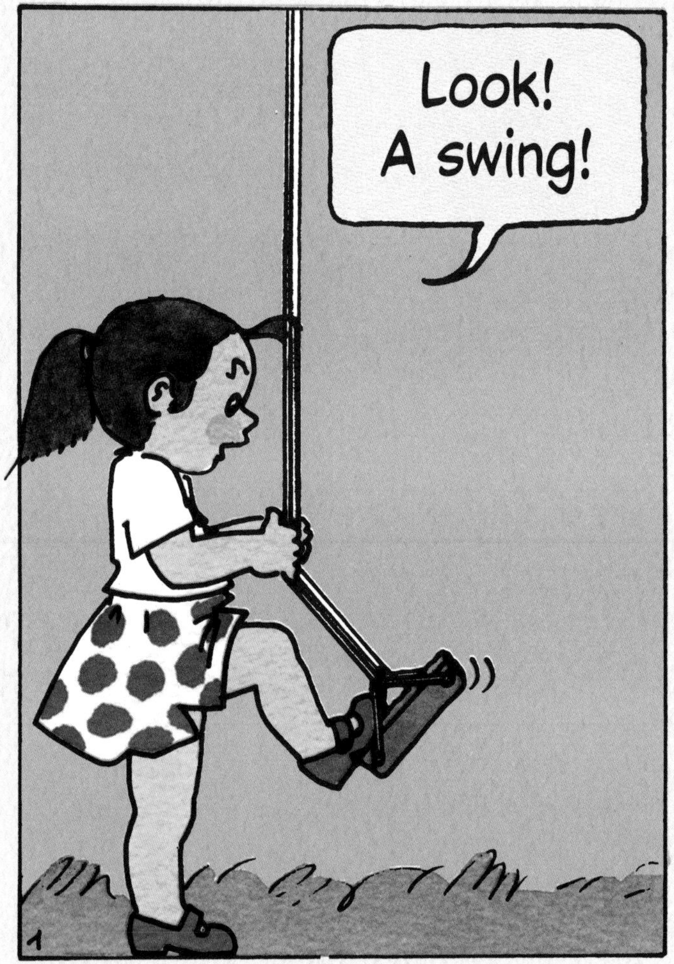
Look!
A swing!
1

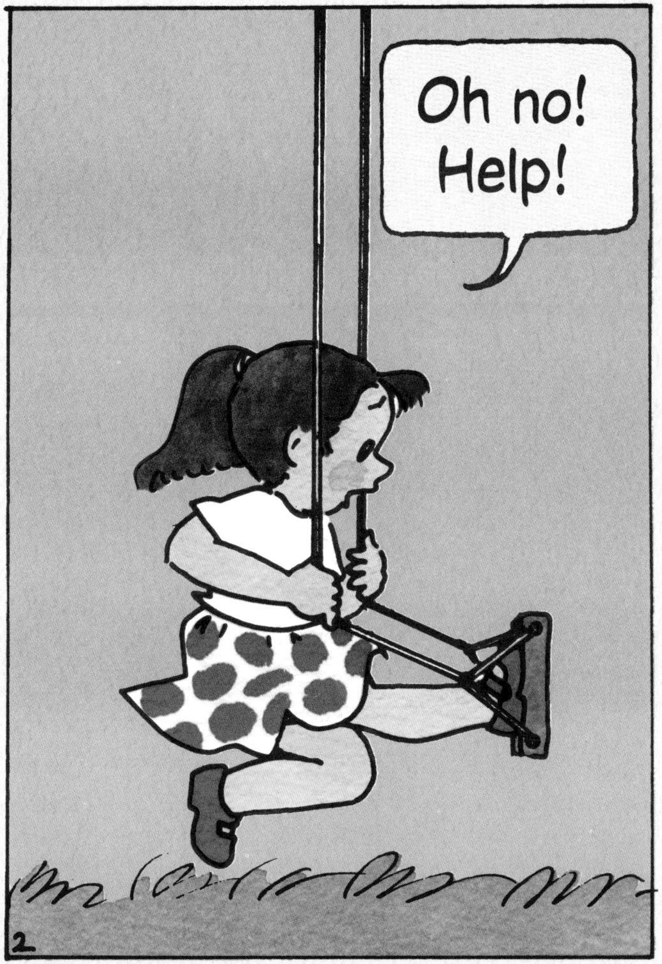
Oh no! Help!

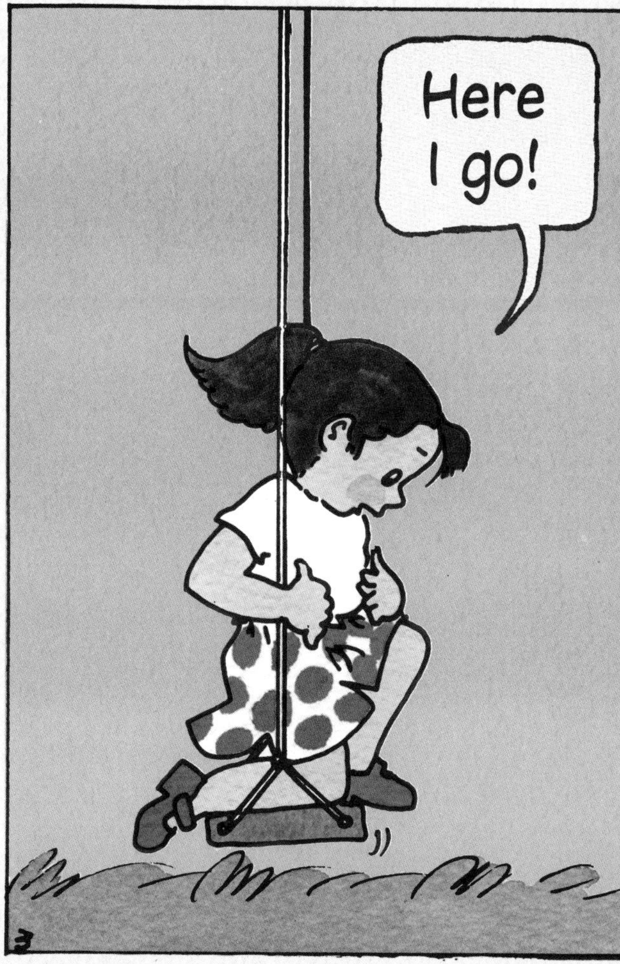
Here I go!

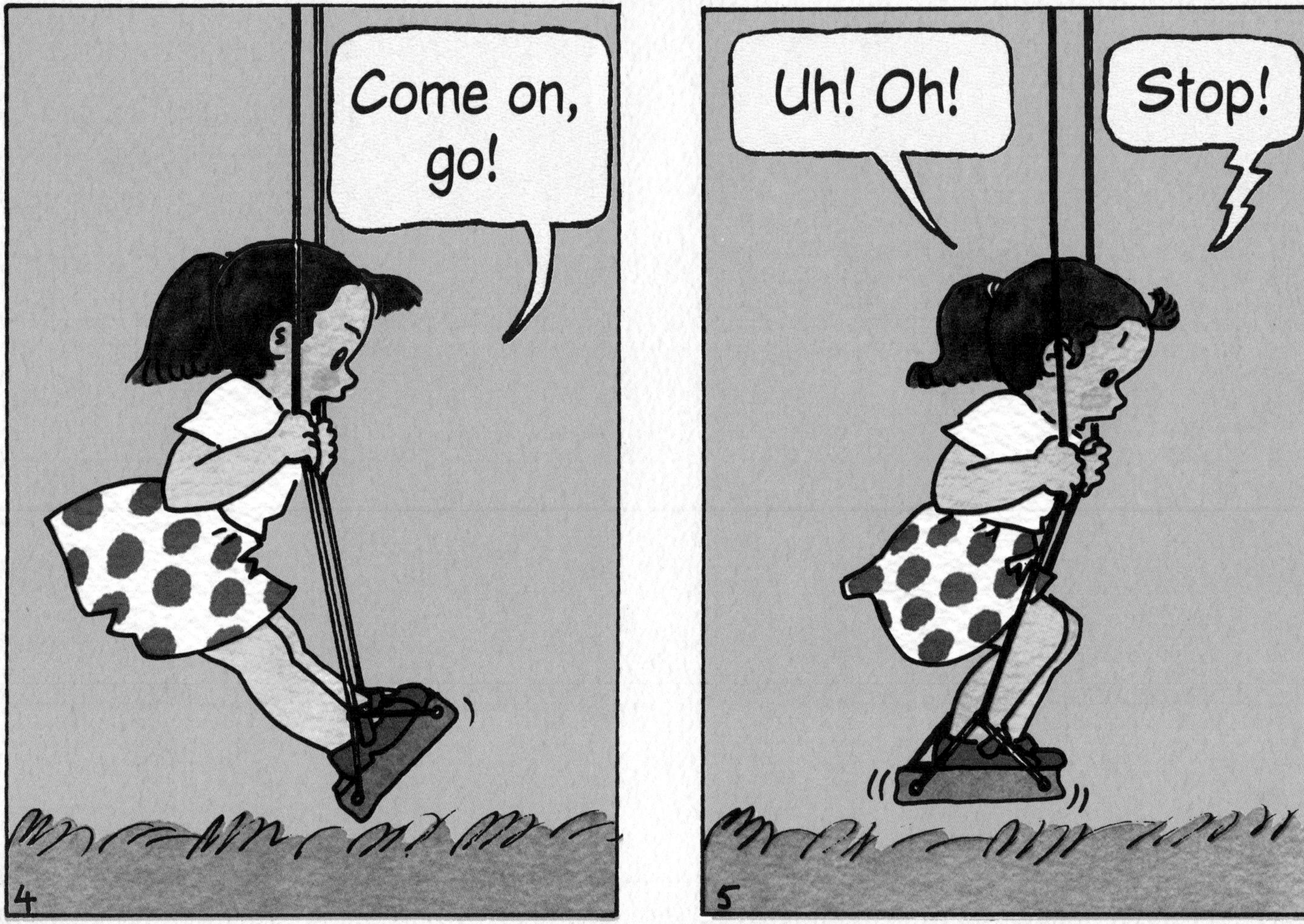
Come on, go!
Uh! Oh!
Stop!

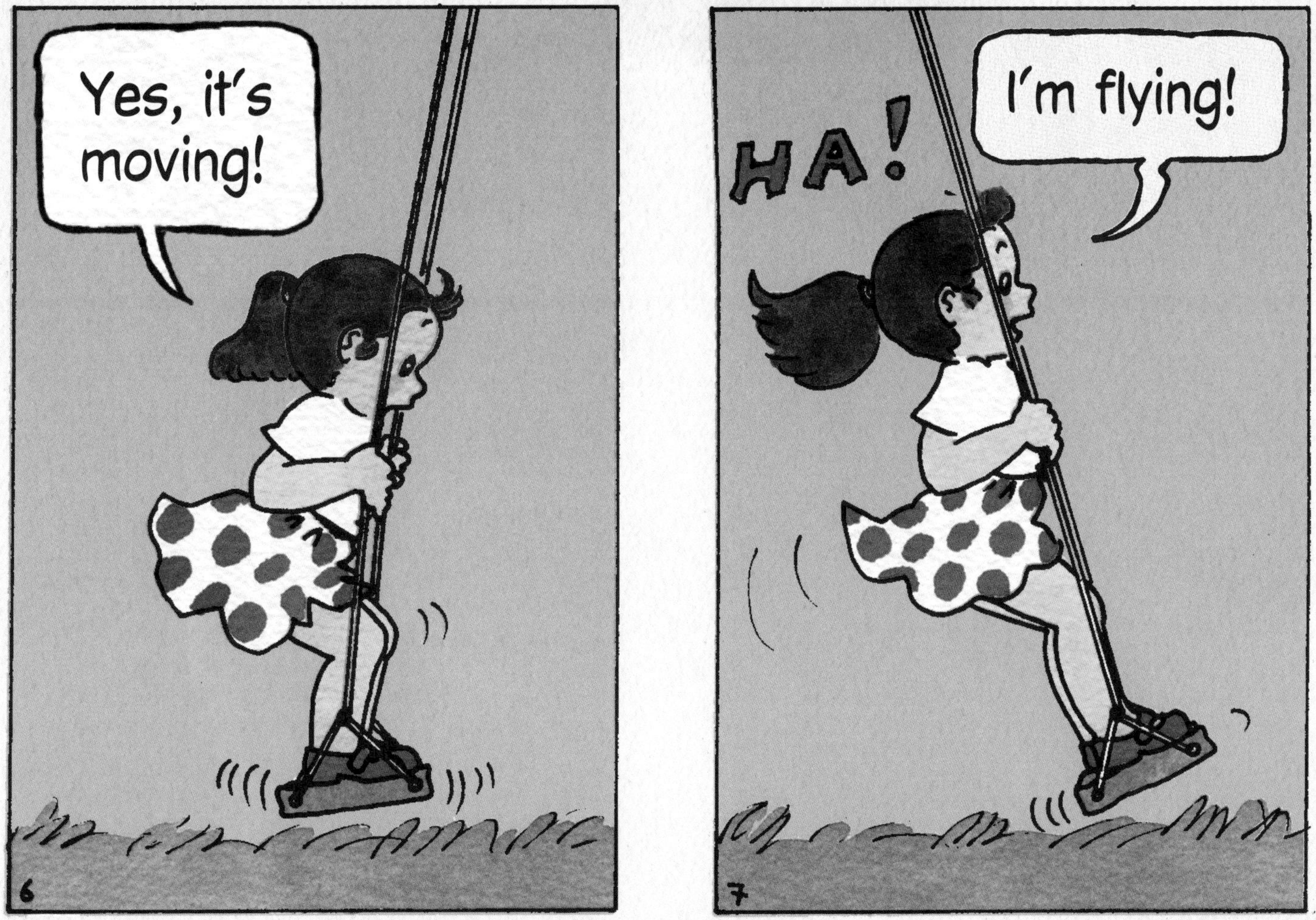
Yes, it's moving!
6
HA!
I'm flying!
7

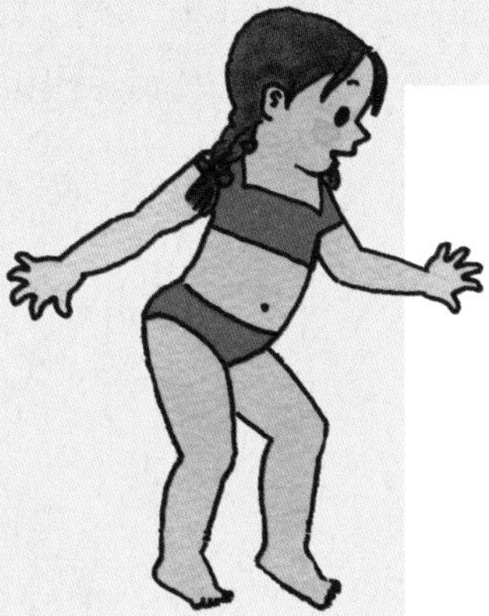

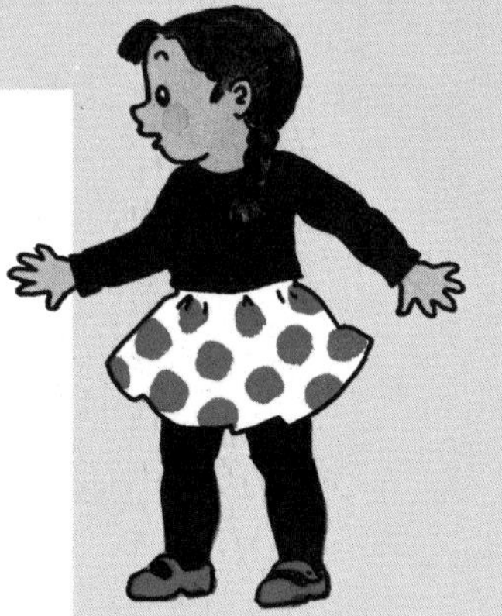

ABOUT THE AUTHOR

Agnès Rosenstiehl is the beloved writer and artist of nearly a hundred children's books, many featuring the deceptively simple antics of "Mimi Cracra," Silly Lilly's French alter ego. In 1995, she received the prestigious Grand Prize for Children's Books from the Société des Gens de Lettres. Agnès formally studied literature as well as music, and is married to an eminent mathematician. She lives in a country house with a garden, hidden in the center of Paris. She has four children and fifteen grandchildren.

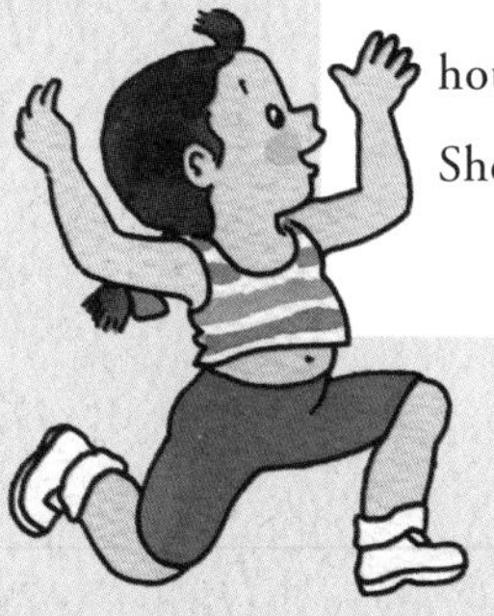

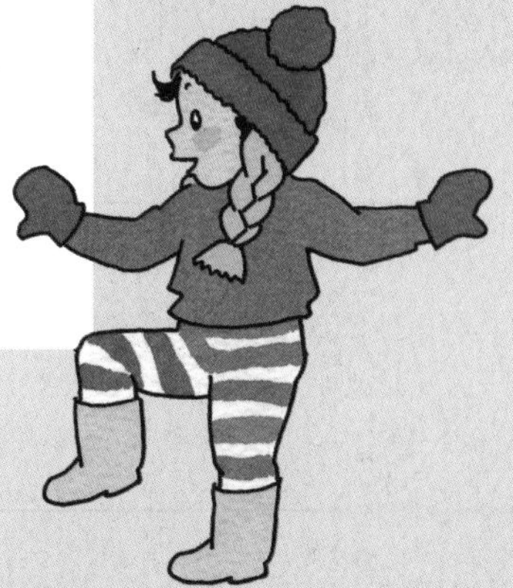

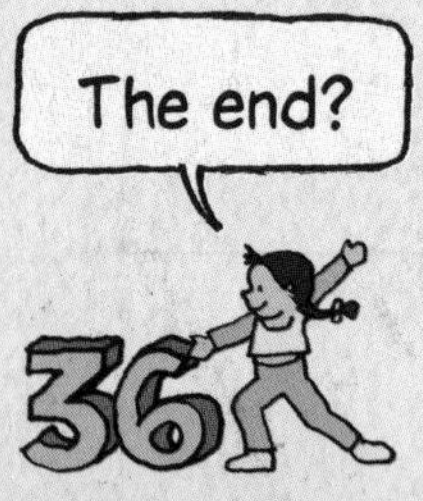
The end?